BABAR
LOSES HIS CROWN

BY LAURENT DE BRUNHOFF

BEGINNER BOOKS   A Division of Random House, Inc.

B C D E F G H I 2 3 4

BABAR

LOSES HIS CROWN

The Babar family is going to Paris.
Everyone is packing bags.
Here are the children—Pom, Flora
and Alexander. Here are Cousin Arthur
and his friend Zephir, the monkey.

Queen Celeste and King Babar
pack their crowns. Babar puts
his crown in a little red bag.

3

Now the Babar family is on the train.
The train is coming into Paris.
"I will show you everything,"
says Babar. "You will love Paris."

Now they are off the train
with all their bags.
The Babar family is waiting
for a taxi.

The taxi takes them to their hotel.

Celeste and the children walk inside.

Babar tells the porter,

"Be careful with that little red bag.

My crown is in it."

In their hotel room, Celeste
opens all the bags. Last of all,
she opens the little red one.
"Look!" she cries.
"What is this? A flute!
Babar! This is not your bag!"

"My crown! It's lost!" cries Babar.
"My crown is gone!"

"I think I know what happened," says
Zephir. "When we were waiting for
the taxi, I saw a man beside us—
a man with a mustache.
He must have taken your bag."

"I need my crown!" says Babar.

"I must wear it tonight!"

"Don't worry," says Celeste.

"We'll find that Mustache-man.

We'll look all over Paris till we do."

So out they go, looking for
the man with Babar's bag.
"He may be up in the Eiffel Tower,"
says Celeste. "All visitors
to Paris go up there."

15

Now they are up in the Eiffel Tower.
But the man with Babar's bag is not.
"Look at the boats down there!"
the children shout.
"Let's go for a ride!"

Babar is sad, but he goes along.
A boat is ready to take off.
"Captain, wait for us!"
shout the children. They climb aboard

The boat is going toward a bridge.
Suddenly Zephir shouts, "Babar, look!
Up on the bridge! The Mustache-man!
He is there with your bag!"

The children all shout, "Captain,
stop! Stop the boat!
Let us off!"

21

BATEAU MOUCHE

The boat does not stop.
So Arthur dives off.
"I'll catch him," he cries.
"I'll catch that Mustache-man!"

Arthur climbs out of the water
just as fast as he can.
He is all wet.
He sees the man with the bag.

Arthur calls to him.

But the man does not hear him.

He is walking away.

Arthur runs after him. He waves.
He yells, "Come back, Mister!
You have Babar's crown!"

But now the man is on a bus.

The bus goes down the street.

Now the Mustache-man is gone.

Arthur is standing in the sun
to dry his clothes. Suddenly
he sees the whole family.
They come running toward him.
"I'm so glad to see you," he says.
"But the red bag—it got away!"

"There's another red bag," shouts
Alexander. He points to a man
sitting on a chair. The man
is giving crumbs to the birds.
"Papa, that bag looks just like yours!"

"Yes, it may be my crown bag,"
Babar says. "But we must be sure
it is the man with the mustache."

They watch the man a long time.
"I'm sure it's the Mustache-man,"
says Zephir.

The Babar family circles around him.

Babar says, "Ahem!"

The man looks up.

He is not the Mustache-man at all!

"Oh, excuse us," says Babar.

"We thought you were someone else."

Now it is noon. It is time for lunch.

Babar takes them to a sidewalk restaurant.

But Babar can't eat.

He is thinking about his crown.

He needs it tonight.

He must wear it to the opera.

But how can he?

He fears his crown is gone forever.

Then Arthur jumps
up from the table.
"There he is!" yells Arthur.
"The man with your crown!"

The man is getting into a red taxi.
He has a little red bag
in his hand. "Quick!" shouts Babar.
"We'll chase him! We'll catch him!"

The Babar family is in two taxis.
"Follow that red one!" they all shout.
A policeman whistles,
but they race right past him.

But now a red light! They have to stop.

They are stuck. They can't move.

The red taxi is gone.

Poor Babar! His crown is lost again.

They get out in front of a market.
"I guess we'll have to forget
about my crown," sighs Babar.
So the children begin to run and play.
They race around.
They hide behind boxes.

Then they see another man
with a small red bag.
All the children rush after him.
Arthur knocks over a box of apples.
Zephir knocks over a box of fish.

46

Now the whole Babar family chases
the man with the bag.
Down the stairs of the subway!
They all follow him, shouting,
"Stop, please, Mr. Mustache!"

Too late! Stuck again!
The gates at the bottom
of the stairs snap shut.

"Bring back my crown!" shouts Babar.
But the man gets on a train,
and the train goes away.

Sadly they come up from the subway.

Babar says nothing.

He is very, very sad.

And the children are very tired.

Celeste says, "We'll put the
children to bed in the hotel.
Then we'll leave them
and go to the opera."

Back in their hotel room,
they say good night to the children.
The three littlest ones
are already half asleep.

Celeste has put on her best dress.
She tells Babar to wear her crown.
"Thank you," he says, "but it's too small.
I will go with no crown at all."

They arrive at the big opera house.
It is all lighted up.
They see hundreds of
people going inside.

"Oh, my," sighs Babar.
"All those people will see me—
ME, the king—without a crown!
I just can't go in there!"

Then, BANG! A man bumps into Babar.

A man with a bag!

The Mustache-man!

Then they open their bags,
and Babar says,
"I can wear a crown.
But I can't wear a flute."
The Mustache-man smiles and says,
"I can play a flute.
But I can't play a crown."

It turns out to be
a great night after all.
The crown is on the head of the King...

...and the flute is under
the Mustache-man's mustache.